The Sleuths of Somerville

MICK'S BURIED TREASURE

The Sleuths of Somerville is published by Stone Arch Books
A Capstone Imprint
1710 Roe Crest Drive
North Mankato, MN 56003
www.mycapstone.com

Library of Congress Cataloging-in-Publication Data
Cataloging-in-publication information is on file with the Library
of Congress.
ISBN 978-1-4965-3178-0 (library binding)
ISBN 978-1-4965-3182-7 (paperback)
ISBN 978-1-4965-3186-5 (eBook PDF)

"A mysterious map leads Jace, Quinn, Astrid, and Rowan on a hunt
for treasure!."—Provided by publisher.

Designer: Tracy McCabe

Illustration Credits: Amerigo Pinelli

Printed and bound in China.
009744F16

The Sleuths of Somerville

MICK'S BURIED TREASURE

by Michele Jakubowski

STONE ARCH BOOKS

a capstone imprint

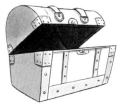

CHAPTER ONE

The Vega kids were beginning to wonder if autumn would ever make its way to Somerville. It was almost the end of September, and the hot summer temperatures were sticking around. Most people were happy about the unseasonably warm weather, but not Rowan and Astrid Vega.

"It has got to be a hundred degrees in that school!" complained 11-year-old Astrid as she sat down at the counter in Mick's Diner, the restaurant owned by her parents, Amelia and Jason Vega.

Her older brother, 12-year-old Rowan, tossed his backpack on an open seat and sat down as well. "No kidding," he said. "They say the school is air conditioned, but the only breeze I've ever felt is from the hand dryer in the bathroom."

Astrid and Rowan were typical siblings. They got along well one minute and were at each other's throats the next. They spent a lot of time together, though, helping out at the diner or hanging out with their best friends, Quinn and Jace.

Neither Astrid nor Rowan had been happy about going back to school, and not just because of the warm temperatures. Their eventful summer had brought Jace and his older sister, Evie, to town after their secret agent parents found themselves in trouble. The town still thought Evie and Jace were mother and son, but the Vegas, Quinn and her parents, and Police Captain Osgood knew the truth. The Vegas had even hired Evie to work in their diner.

Jace had become fast friends with Rowan, Astrid, and Quinn. The foursome had spent the rest of the summer looking for adventure and solving mysteries. Now that school had started, they'd had little time for much else besides homework.

Astrid and Rowan sat glumly at the counter staring at their books. It wasn't long before Jace and Quinn joined them.

The four of them must have looked pretty pathetic. When Mr. Vega saw them sitting there, he asked, "What's going on here? Is the Frowny Face Convention in town?" He shaped his mouth into an exaggerated frown and added, "Can I join your frown fest?"

Astrid tried to contain the smile that crossed her face. "Not funny, Dad!"

Mrs. Vega made her way over and asked, "How was your day, kids? Anything exciting happen at school?"

"About the most exciting thing that happened was when Tyler Shepard split his pants in math class and had to go home early," Rowan snorted.

Then he looked up as if he'd just had a great idea. "Hey, Mom, do you have any of my old pants from last year?"

Mrs. Vega smiled and shook her head. "Nice try."

"How about you girls, anything exciting as split pants happen to you today?" Mr. Vega asked Astrid and Quinn.

"I wish," Astrid replied. "All we got was a huge assignment for school."

"Oh yeah? What's it about?" asked Mrs. Vega.

"Thanks to that letter, and everyone's sudden interest in our town's history, we now have to write a report about our family and how we came to live in Somerville," Astrid said.

Over the summer, a letter of historic importance written by former President Abraham Lincoln had been found in the Somerville Museum. After much debate about selling the letter, the residents were persuaded by Miss Coco, the town's oldest living resident, to keep the letter and display it with pride. The situation had sparked curiosity about anything to do with Somerville's past and made the museum a popular place.

"That sounds interesting!" Mrs. Vega said.

"I'm glad you think so, because I have to interview you and Dad to get information," Astrid replied.

"I can tell you this," Mr. Vega said. "When we rolled into Somerville, we didn't plan on being here any longer than the time it took to fill up our gas tank."

"Really?" asked Quinn. "What made you stay?"

With a big smile, Mrs. Vega said, "A man named Mick."

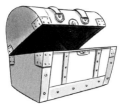

CHAPTER TWO

"It all started during one of the worst blizzards in New York's history," Mr. Vega began as he leaned back on the counter, settling in to tell his story. "Sixteen inches had already come down and the storm wasn't even halfway over! The roads were a mess and many of them were shut down completely. My parents almost didn't make it to the hospital—"

"Oh no, Dad! Not again!" Rowan interrupted. "It's bad enough that we have to listen to that story every year on your birthday!"

Jace and Quinn looked confused, so Astrid had to fill them in.

"Long story short: My dad was born in the middle of a blizzard, and my grandma almost didn't make it to the hospital," Astrid said in a monotone voice. "Fascinating stuff."

"It's a great story!" Mr. Vega protested. "Wait until you hear the part about our car spinning out on the freeway!"

Mrs. Vega smiled as she gently patted her husband on the shoulder. "Why don't we skip ahead about twenty years to the part they actually asked to hear about?"

Mr. Vega crossed his arms and shrugged. "Okay, but then they're going to miss the part about me hitting a grand slam in Little League when I was nine and getting the lead in my high school's production of *Fiddler on the Roof*."

"I think they'll survive," Mrs. Vega told her husband before turning toward the foursome.

"The story of how we ended up in Somerville began the summer we graduated from college," she told them. "We got married in June and decided to relocate to San Francisco, where some of our friends were moving. Even though we had never been any farther west than Chicago, we were excited about starting our new lives in a new city. We packed up everything we owned and hit the road in your dad's old pickup truck. That thing was so ancient. It's a miracle we made it out of New York!"

"That old truck was the best!" Mr. Vega said. "Besides, if we didn't need to stop for gas and to check the oil every hundred miles, we might have driven right past Somerville!"

"That's true." Mrs. Vega nodded. "And if Earl at the gas station hadn't suggested we get a bite to eat at the diner, we never would have met Mick."

"Mick was such a character!" Mr. Vega told them. "We sat right at this very counter and listened to his stories as we ate the most amazing meal. Before we knew it, several hours had passed, and it was dark out. We decided to stay the night and head out of town the next morning. We checked in to Mrs. Cheever's hotel across the street."

"Of course we couldn't leave without breakfast," Mrs. Vega continued. "Of course we came back to Mick's for breakfast the next morning. I'd never had such delicious eggs! Mick told me if I stayed around until the breakfast rush ended, he'd show me how he made them. Mick knew how to make everything, and he kept teaching me new tricks. I hung out with him in the kitchen right up until the lunch rush started. I was having so much fun, I stayed and helped him."

"And you know how friendly the people in Somerville are," Mr. Vega added. "I stood at the counter all day chatting and refilling coffees. By the end of the day, Mick had offered us both jobs, and we decided to stay for a while."

The other customers began listening, and soon they were reminiscing about Mick.

"He sure was a great guy," Mr. Goodwin said. "He had customers who only came through town once or twice a year, and no matter how long it had been he greeted them by name. It was as if they'd been in the day before."

Mrs. Chen nodded and added, "Mick was so kind. If he knew a family in town was struggling, he always made sure they had something to eat, and without calling any attention to it."

"He was also a matchmaker," Mrs. Studebaker said with a grin on her face. "I think half of the marriages in this town started when Mick sat people near each other at the diner. Even though we went to school together, I had never even spoken to my husband until Mick introduced us at this very counter. He was such a romantic!"

"So, where is Mick now?" Jace asked innocently.

The mood of the room suddenly shifted. The jovial atmosphere turned dark.

"Well," Mrs. Vega sighed. "After we'd been working here for almost a year, Mick asked us if we would take care of things so he could finally go on a vacation. He hadn't left Somerville since he'd opened the diner, and he wanted to do some traveling. He said he wanted to see the world before he got too old."

Tears came to Mrs. Vega's eyes. Mr. Vega put his arm around his wife as he picked up the story. "He rented an RV and set out. We got postcards from him every few weeks from all over the country. He was having an incredible time and kept extending his trip. That was fine with us. We loved running the diner."

"After a while, the time between postcards grew longer and longer," Mr. Vega continued, "until the next thing we heard was from a lawyer in Watertown. Mick had passed and had left the diner to us in his will." Mr. Vega paused and cleared his throat in an attempt to hold back the tears. In a softer voice he added, "So, that's the story of how we came to Somerville."

The diner was silent as they all remembered their old friend, Mick.

Finally, Miss Coco broke the silence. "And what about that pie?"

Everyone smiled. Nearly everyone, that is.

"Pie?" Jace was confused. "What pie?"

"Mick used to make the best cherry pie in the whole world," Mrs. Vega said.

"Too bad you'll never be able to have a piece," Mr. Reynolds said to Jace. "Mick used a secret recipe and refused to share it with anyone."

"I tried for years to re-create that pie, but I never came close," Mrs. Vega said, shaking her head. "I finally gave up and focused on donuts."

"That Mick liked to keep you guessing," Mayor Arnold said. "He had his secret recipes, and he was a joker, too. Every now and then he'd add blue food coloring to the mashed potatoes or put sugar in one of the salt shakers."

Mrs. Iceman chuckled, adding, "How about when he used to add things to the menu to see if we were paying attention? My favorite was 'Free Tomato with Every Bacon and Lettuce Sandwich.'"

"Remember when he convinced everyone that he had buried a treasure somewhere in town?" asked Mr. Rossi. "He pulled that stunt right before he left on his trip."

The words "buried" and "treasure" got the attention of Rowan, Astrid, Jace, and Quinn. While the adults continued trading stories about Mick, the four friends immediately exchanged glances. They had to find out more.

"What's this about a buried treasure?" Astrid asked her mom.

Mrs. Vega waved her hand dismissively. "Oh, that's Mick for you," she said. "Before he went on his trip he left a single clue and said that anyone who could figure out all the clues would find a buried treasure at the end. No one got very far. We all figured it was just another one of his practical jokes and he was trying to get us to run around town like a bunch of fools."

Rowan, Jace, Quinn, and Astrid exchanged glances again. Rowan smiled at his friends. Buried treasure, huh? It sounded like they just found their next mystery!

"Do you still have that clue?" Rowan asked.

Mrs. Vega thought for a moment before saying, "I think I do. But you're wasting your time. I doubt there is any buried treasure to be found."

The foursome smiled at each other. They'd see about that!

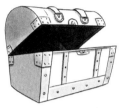

CHAPTER THREE

Mrs. Vega agreed to look for Mick's buried treasure clue, but only if the four of them got their homework done first. With lightning speed, they plowed through their math equations and social studies worksheets.

They found Mrs. Vega in her office, a room located off the diner's kitchen. It was small but very neat and organized. Mrs. Vega was sitting at her desk, looking at some pictures. Papers and photos spilled out of an open box on the desk.

"Just look how young we were." Mrs. Vega sighed as she showed them an old photo from the pile. A younger-looking Mr. and Mrs. Vega stood on either side of an old man with shaggy white hair and a long beard.

"Is that Mick?" asked Quinn.

With a smile on her face and a tear in her eye, Mrs. Vega nodded. "Yep, that's Mick."

Rowan looked closer. "Add about fifty pounds and he'd kind of look like Santa Claus."

They all laughed.

"He was as kind and jolly as Santa Claus," Mrs. Vega said, wiping the tear from her eye. "Okay, enough walking down memory lane. I'm almost certain I put that clue in this box."

Mrs. Vega rummaged through the box for a moment before pulling something from the bottom.

"Here it is!" she said.

Mrs. Vega held up a small scroll, and then she unrolled it. The yellowed paper had been singed along the edges.

"Fancy!" Astrid said.

The foursome gathered around as Mrs. Vega laid the paper flat on the desk. In a curvy script in thick black ink, it read:

I leave to you, my dear old friend
A treasure hunt with a very sweet end!
While I travel the country, far and wide
A prized possession for you I did hide.
My clues are clear, I've left out no detail.
To get this hunt started, just call me . . .

"'Call me'?" Astrid was confused already. "How can we call him?"

Mrs. Vega shook her head as she put the other items back into the box. "You guys are the detectives. I'm sure you can figure it out."

She returned the box to its place on a shelf and left the office.

They read and reread the clue. Rowan read it aloud to see if that would help. He repeated the last line very slowly: "To get this hunt started, just call me . . ."

"Ishmael!" Jace exclaimed.

Rowan, Quinn, and Astrid looked at their friend as if he'd gone crazy.

"Excuse me?" Astrid asked.

"Ishmael!" Jace said, a big smile on his face. "It rhymes, doesn't it?"

"Yes, but it still doesn't make any sense," Rowan said. "I mean, I could make up lots of words that rhyme with 'detail.'"

"Yeah, like 'schmeetail' and 'retail,'" Astrid said.

"Um, 'retail' is a real word," Quinn said, rolling her eyes.

"Whatever," Astrid replied with exasperation. "You see what I mean!"

Jace shook his head. "I didn't make it up! 'Call me Ishmael.' It's the first line in a famous book. *Moby Dick,* I think."

Quinn looked surprised. "You've read *Moby Dick*?" she asked.

"Well, no," Jace replied sheepishly. "I knew that from a trivia game I used to play all the time. It was such a funny name that it stuck with me."

"Well, we've got nothing else to go on." Rowan sighed. "Do you know anything else about this book? Does it have anything to do with treasure hunts?"

Jace shrugged. "I have no idea."

"Why don't we go to the library and see what we can find out?" Quinn suggested.

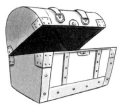

CHAPTER FOUR

Mick's Diner was located on Main Street, which ran about a mile before looping around the town square and heading back toward the highway. The buildings that surrounded the square were some of the oldest in Somerville, and they included the city hall and the town's library.

Martha Somer, the wife of town founder Albert J. Somer, had been an avid reader and insisted that the library be one of the first buildings built. Martha was an only child born into a very wealthy family, and her father happily funded the building of the Martha Westfield Somer Library. Now known simply as the Somerville Library, it was one of the nicest buildings in town, with tall, stained glass windows and marble floors.

"Whoa," Jace said in awe as they entered the building. "Who knew there was such a fancy building like this in little ol' Somerville?"

"You would if you picked up a book every once in a while," said Astrid.

They made their way to the information desk, where Mrs. Sager, the librarian, told them where they could find a copy of *Moby Dick*. After locating the correct shelf, they needed only a moment to find two copies of Herman Melville's classic book.

Astrid removed one copy from the shelf while Rowan grabbed the other.

"What, exactly, are we looking for?" Astrid asked.

Rowan shrugged. "I have no idea, but hopefully we can find something useful in one of these books."

Rowan slowly opened the book. When he didn't find anything on the inside cover, he carefully flipped through the pages.

"Nothing here," he said with a frown.

Astrid opened her copy and noticed writing on the inside cover.

"Look!" she said excitedly. In a tight script in all caps, the book read:

DAER LLEW EB TSUM UOY RETNUH RIAF YM
BOJ DOOG

?DEF LLEW UOY ERA SI UOY OT NOITSEUQ
TXEN YM

TI KRAP OT EVAH YAM UOY RAC YB LEVART
UOY FI

TEKRAM EHT TA DNOUF EB NAC KEES UOY
EULC TXEN EHT ROF

HCAER FO TUO LLITS S'TI TUB RESOLC
GNITTEG ER'UOY

?HCAEP A HTIW TRATS UOY TSEGGUS I THGIM

"Is that a foreign language?" asked Astrid.

"If it is, it's none that I've ever seen," replied Jace who, having traveled around the world with his parents, was a reliable source.

Quinn took the book from Astrid and studied the writing closer. After a moment she said, "Let me try something."

The others followed her as she walked away. Rowan and Jace stopped just before following her into the women's restroom.

"I guess we'll wait out here," Rowan said as his cheeks turned red.

While they waited, Jace playfully shoved Rowan. "You almost went in the girls' bathroom," he teased.

Rowan shoved him back. "So did you!"

They were still standing outside of the restrooms when a group of kids from school walked by.

"Hey, Rowan!" said Dirk Turner, the group's unofficial leader.

"Hey! What's up, Dirk?" Rowan replied as they performed an intricate handshake.

"Hey, Dirk!" Jace said cheerfully.

"Hey," Dirk mumbled coolly without looking in Jace's direction. "So Rowan, a bunch of us are going to the movies tomorrow night. They're showing a double feature of *Mutant Zombies from Outer Space 1* and *2*. Want to come along?"

"Maybe," Rowan replied. His thoughts were focused on their treasure hunt, not his favorite movies. "I'll let you know what we've got going on."

"Well, if *you* want to come along, let me know," Dirk said, pointing at Rowan. He began to walk away and added, "See you, Rowan."

The rest of the boys trailed behind Dirk, each of them saying goodbye to Rowan. It was impossible to miss the fact that no one acknowledged Jace.

"That was weird," Rowan said. He didn't know why they were acting so rudely.

Jace thought he knew why, but he didn't say anything. He had been looking forward to starting at a new school and making friends. Somerville was starting to feel like the home he'd never had before.

He had never made friends like Rowan, Quinn, and Astrid. He liked the idea of getting to know the kids they had talked about, and seen here and there, all summer.

The kids at Somerville Middle School weren't used to change. At first, some of them had been welcoming, but once Dirk decided he didn't like Jace, the other guys all followed suit. Jace hadn't said anything to Rowan because he was hoping it would get better as the other kids got to know him. After the way Dirk and the others acted in front of Rowan, though, he knew it was a hopeless cause.

Rowan saw the look on Jace's face and felt bad. "They're just not used to new people," he explained. "Ninety-nine percent of the kids at school were born and raised in Somerville. Just give them a chance to get to know you. It'll be fine."

"I guess," Jace mumbled.

They were both glad when Astrid and Quinn threw open the restroom door.

"We got it!" Quinn said, beaming.

"Got what?" asked Rowan.

"A chocolate chip cookie," Astrid said sarcastically. "The next clue, you goof! What else would we be talking about?"

Rowan blushed again.

"So tell us what it says already!" Jace said, happy to have something else to think about besides his unpopularity.

Quinn looked at the book and said, "It says, 'Good job my fair hunter, you must be well read. My next question for you is, 'Are you well fed?' If you travel by car you may have to park it, for the next clue you seek can be found at the market. You're getting closer, but it's still out of reach. Might I suggest you start with a peach?'"

"Are you sure?" Rowan asked. "How did you figure that out?"

Quinn smiled proudly. "It was written backwards. All we had to do was hold it up to the mirror."

"Nice," Rowan said, high-fiving Quinn. "Two clues down!"

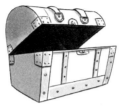

CHAPTER FIVE

The following day, Rowan and Astrid raced home from school to finish their homework. They were anxious to head over to Goodwin's Market. They planned to meet Jace and Quinn and search for their next clue.

As they were leaving the diner, they told their mom where they were going. "Good luck," she said with the same mischievous grin she'd worn when they were heading to the library the day before.

Astrid looked suspiciously at her mom. "Does that smile mean we're headed in the right direction?" she asked. Then she frowned. "Or that we read the clue wrong? Do you know something we don't know? Of course you do! Why else would you be smiling like that? What do you know? Tell me!"

"Settle down, spaz," Rowan said to his sister. "She's just messing with you. Let's get out of here before she gets any further into your head."

Mrs. Vega wiggled her eyebrows. "Bye!" she sang playfully, waving over her shoulder as she headed back toward her office.

Astrid and Rowan found Jace and Quinn waiting for them in front of the market. Before they could say hello, Jace started talking.

"We were just trying to figure out how to find the next clue," he said. "What do you think he meant by 'start with a peach'?"

"I don't know. I was thinking that maybe we could ask Mr. or Mrs. Goodwin if they know anything about a clue," Rowan suggested.

As much as she didn't like admitting her brother was right, Astrid said, "Good idea."

The foursome headed into Goodwin's Market, where they found Mrs. Goodwin standing behind the customer service counter.

"Hello, kids," she said with a smile. "Did your folks send you in to get something for the diner?"

"Not today, Mrs. Goodwin," Astrid replied. "We're here for something else."

Rowan explained. "We're looking for clues that Mick left behind for a treasure hunt. The last one we found led us here."

Mrs. Goodwin's eyes lit up. "Oh, Mick! Such a card! I know exactly what you're talking about. You must be doing well so far on the hunt."

"It's been fun," Quinn told her. "We gathered from the last clue that we are supposed to come here."

"It said something about a peach," Astrid added.

"Oh, yes," Mrs. Goodwin chuckled. "I can show you the clue, but I have to warn you: most people who went on this so-called treasure hunt gave up after finding this clue. I'm pretty sure it was just a practical joke. Mick was the town's biggest prankster."

They didn't like the sound of that and exchanged worried glances as they followed Mrs. Goodwin to the produce section.

Mrs. Goodwin talked as she led them. "I don't even know how he did it. Mick somehow managed to leave a clue on the bottom of the peach display without anyone seeing him do it. I sure do miss that crazy guy!"

All of the fruit was displayed in wooden boxes propped up at an angle. As they reached the peaches, Mrs. Goodwin instructed them, "One of you will have to crawl under there to see the clue. It's scratched on the bottom. Be careful. If you bump it too hard, we'll have peaches everywhere!"

The foursome exchanged glances until Astrid finally said, "Oh fine! I'll do it!"

The others weren't sure about the clumsiest one of them performing the task, but no one else wanted to volunteer, either.

Astrid crouched down and carefully scooted under the display. She was quiet for a moment before exclaiming, "I see it!"

Quinn slid her a piece of paper and a pencil and said, "Here, write it down exactly as you see it."

A moment later, Astrid shimmied out from under the display and stood up, proud of herself for not overturning all of the fruit.

"What did it say?" Rowan asked impatiently, grabbing the paper from his sister. He glanced down and said, "Is that it?"

On the paper Astrid had written: "A) 12."

"I looked all over. That's all that was down there," Astrid said with a frown. "I wrote it down exactly as it was written."

Mrs. Goodwin patted Astrid's back and said, "Now you see why most people stopped at this clue."

Jace looked at the others. "What do we do now?" he asked.

Rowan shook his head. "I have no idea. I guess we try to figure out what it means."

They stood in frustrated silence for a moment before Mrs. Goodwin reached over and grabbed some peaches. She handed one to each of them and said, "Here, you deserve a peach. I know it's not buried treasure, but it's something!"

They mumbled their appreciation and headed out. Out front they sat on the curb eating their peaches.

"'A) 12'?" Jace said, wiping peach juice from his mouth. "What does that even mean?"

"It doesn't make any sense," Quinn said glumly.

As they were pondering the clue some more, Dirk and a few other kids walked by.

"Doesn't this look like a good time?" Dirk said. "Eating peaches on the curb. What a fun night!"

"Hey, Dirk," Rowan said without any enthusiasm.

"So, Rowan, are you up for the movies? We're heading over now," Dirk asked.

"No, I can't," Rowan replied.

"Too busy eating peaches?" Dirk asked. The others with him laughed as if he'd said the funniest thing they'd ever heard.

As much as she liked doing it herself, Astrid didn't like it when other people teased her brother. She blurted out, "He's busy figuring out a clue on a treasure hunt, okay?"

Rowan glared at her, and Astrid knew she'd made a mistake mentioning the treasure hunt.

"A treasure hunt?" Dirk asked.

"Um, well, sort of," Rowan mumbled. "Not really. I think we hit a dead end, so . . ."

"Sure," Dirk replied. He shot a mean look at Jace before adding, "When you're done hanging with the little kids and the losers, let me know."

As Dirk and his friends walked away, Astrid asked Rowan, "What was that all about? When did Dirk become so mean?"

Rowan shrugged, not wanting to make Jace feel uncomfortable. "I don't know. Maybe he's just in a bad mood."

"Aren't we all?" Quinn said with a snort, and the four of them went back to eating their peaches in silence.

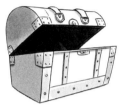

CHAPTER SIX

The following day the foursome was hanging out at Jace's house, formerly known as the Potters' place, after school. They were all still grouchy and frustrated at their inability to figure out the latest clue.

"I couldn't stop thinking about that clue all day," Quinn told the others as they gathered around the large island in the home's spacious kitchen for a snack.

They laughed now about how afraid Quinn, Rowan, and Astrid had been when they went into the Potters' place for the first time. Years of stories about the home's original owners had made them uneasy. Although the house had been beautifully remodeled inside, there was still an air of mystery about both it and Mr. P., the man who had brought Jace and Evie to Somerville.

Jace grabbed some granola bars, cheese crackers, and pretzels from the pantry. As he set them on the island he said, "Me either. In math, Mr. Greene said if I didn't stop daydreaming he'd send me down to Mrs. Iceman's office."

"Well, thanks to Astrid's big mouth, I had Dirk following me around all day asking about the treasure hunt," Rowan complained.

At the mention of Dirk's name, Jace's mouth went dry. The cheese crackers he was chewing suddenly felt like paste. He turned around to get a glass of water and hoped that his friends didn't notice how uncomfortable he had become. He knew that Rowan was a good friend, but he was beginning to worry that now that school had started, Dirk may try to get between them. The thought made Jace feel awful.

Rowan went on, "Dirk says he wants to help us with the treasure hunt. Nice going, Astrid."

Astrid threw her hands up defensively and said, "I'm sorry for trying to stick up for you. Trust me, I'll never do it again."

Rowan rolled his eyes. "If Dirk helps, we'll have to split the treasure with him. If we say no, he might look for it himself and get to the treasure first. Then all of this work will be for nothing."

Astrid grumbled under her breath, "It already feels like it's for nothing."

Astrid felt bad about telling Dirk and his friends about the treasure hunt. She knew Rowan was right, and that made her feel even worse. She grabbed the paper they had written all of the clues on and went to sit by herself in the living room.

Rowan unwrapped a second granola bar and shoved half of it in his mouth. "I don't know what the

'A' means, but I was thinking about the 'twelve.'"
He stopped to swallow his bite and immediately
stuffed the other half of granola bar in his mouth.
He gulped the big bite down and continued.
"Another way to say 'twelve' is 'a dozen,' right? I
wonder if it has something to do with the word
'dozen.'"

Quinn nodded her head. "Maybe it's referring
to a baker's dozen? Maybe the next clue is at the
bakery or the Sugar Shack?"

Rowan nodded his head slowly as he pondered
what Quinn had said. It didn't make a lot of sense,
but they had no other leads. "The Sugar Shack
wasn't open when Mick left town, so it wouldn't be
there," he said. "Maybe it's at the diner? My mom
makes a lot of baked goods."

Jace looked confused. "Isn't a baker's dozen
actually thirteen? If the clue had to do with baked
goods, wouldn't it say 'thirteen'?"

Quinn shook her head. "That doesn't make any
sense! Why would a baker's dozen mean thirteen?

Everyone knows a dozen is twelve. We learned that in math."

In the other room, Astrid peeked her head up over the couch. "Hey, guys?" she called.

The others were too busy arguing to hear her. "Maybe there's thirteen in a baker's dozen so the baker has one to eat?" Jace reasoned. He may have been daydreaming in math class, but he was certain that a baker's dozen meant thirteen.

Astrid looked again at the clues. She sat up a little more. "Guys?" she said a little louder.

"So what you're saying is that for every twelve cookies a baker makes, he has to eat one?" Quinn argued. "That's ridiculous!"

"That does sound pretty weird," Rowan said.

Jace was exasperated. "I'm telling you! A baker's dozen is a thing, and it means thirteen! I'm sure of it!"

Astrid had had enough of the silly bickering. Studying the clues had made her notice something they had overlooked. She stood up on the couch and shouted, "Guys! Enough about the cookies! I found something!"

Rowan, Jace, and Quinn fell silent, a bit embarrassed by their ridiculous fight.

Rowan sighed and walked over to the couch. "Well, it's got to be better than talking about fat bakers," he grumbled.

When they were gathered around, Astrid showed them the clues. "I was reading these again and something jumped out at me. The clue in the book says, 'Might I suggest you start with a peach.'"

"And we did start with a peach," Rowan said with annoyance. "What are you saying?"

"*Start,*" Astrid, emphasizing the word. "Maybe that means there are other clues under the rest of the fruit displays? Maybe the 'A' means there is a 'B,' 'C,' and 'D'?"

Rowan's jaw dropped. He said something he very rarely said to his little sister: "That totally makes sense!"

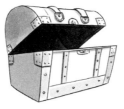

CHAPTER SEVEN

When Rowan, Jace, Astrid, and Quinn got back to Goodwin's Market, they were surprised by the number of cars filling the parking lot.

"Wow," Astrid said. "This place is hoppin'."

As they entered, they saw that the market was full of people and immediately picked up on a festive mood. The customers casually pushed their carts around and stopped to socialize with other shoppers.

Today no one was in their typical rush to get their groceries and head out.

Quinn laughed. "Who knew Goodwin's Market was the place to be on a Friday night?"

They also noticed that they were, by far, the youngest people in the market. "Yeah, it's the place to be if you're over forty!" Jace added.

Mr. Goodwin stood near a display of canned vegetables and chatted with some customers. The foursome made their way over and waited patiently for him to finish his conversation. When the customers finally moved on, Mr. Goodwin seemed surprised to see them there.

"Something I can help you find?" he asked.

Rowan leaned in, speaking quietly so they wouldn't be overheard. "We were in the other day looking for clues in Mick's treasure hunt. Would it be okay if we looked under some of the other fruit displays for more clues?"

Mr. Goodwin glanced at the produce department, which was packed with people. He frowned. "I'm not sure that now would be a good time to go climbing under the displays. Do you think you could come back later?"

They exchanged glances, each one of them anxious to see if Astrid had been right about more clues. "Would it be okay if we hung out until it was less busy?" Rowan asked.

Mr. Goodwin could tell by the looks on their faces how important it was to them. He nodded. "Okay, things should quiet down in about an hour."

As they thanked him, a page came over the PA system: "Clean up in aisle three!"

"Better go," Mr. Goodwin said as he headed in the direction of aisle three.

Astrid, Quinn, Jace, and Rowan stood near the canned vegetable display, confused and frustrated. "Why is the market so busy?" Astrid wondered aloud. "It's a Friday night."

"Because it's sample night, silly!" Miss Coco said as she pushed her cart around the corner. "It's the best night of the week to shop."

All four of them noticed that the only thing in Miss Coco's cart was her purse. No one said a word, and they must have looked unconvinced by her explanation. She waved her hand and said, "Come on, I'll show you."

They followed Miss Coco away from the produce department. As they turned the corner they saw a stand with a crowd of people around it.

"Ohhh!" Miss Coco proclaimed excitedly. "It must be something good!"

As the people took their samples and walked away, the foursome and Miss Coco made their way to the front.

"Would you like to try some gourmet pizza?" said a smiling woman wearing a Goodwin's Market apron.

They each took a slice served on a napkin and stepped away.

"This is almost a full-sized piece!" Quinn said before taking a bite.

They continued to follow Miss Coco around the market. Along the way they enjoyed chips and salsa, frozen yogurt, and organic apple juice. After a little prompting, they were pleasantly surprised to find out they all liked kale chips.

Down the next aisle an even larger crowd was gathered around a woman cooking up something in a skillet. Delicious smells wafted through the air.

"I feel like I'm watching a cooking show on TV," Jace whispered to Rowan.

Miss Coco indicated that they should move along. "The cooking demonstrations take too long," she explained. "Plus, all you get is a small sample and coupons for the ingredients."

They walked along the aisles and enjoyed samples of vegetable dip on crackers, trail mix, and mozzarella sticks before ending up back at the produce department. Luckily, that area had mostly cleared out.

"I'm stuffed," said Jace, patting his belly.

"I am, too," Quinn said, groaning. "And now I know why my mom likes to grocery shop by herself on Friday nights!"

Still in a sampling mood, Miss Coco plucked a grape from the fruit display and popped it in her mouth. "I think I'll head home and take a nap," she said. "You kids have a good night."

Astrid noticed her still-empty shopping cart. "Don't you need groceries?" she asked.

Miss Coco waved her hand and said, "Heavens, no! I'm too full to think about food!"

As the last of the shoppers left the produce area, Rowan got permission from Mr. Goodwin to check under the displays. They decided to each look under a different display to save time. They carefully slid under the fruit displays, and within minutes they came back out with smiles on their faces.

In order to not draw any attention to themselves, they hurriedly made their way out of the market to compare their findings. They gathered under a tree at the far edge of the parking lot and laid out their notes.

"I can't believe you were right," Rowan said to Astrid as he shook his head in astonishment.

"Gee, thanks," Astrid replied sarcastically.

On individual pieces of paper they had written: "D) 83," "B) 34 Main," and "C) Box 13."

"If you include the first clue and put them in order, they read '1234 Main Box 1383,'" Rowan said.

"Isn't 1234 Main Street the address for the post office?" asked Quinn.

Rowan nodded and smiled. "Yep, and I bet our next clue is waiting for us in box 1383."

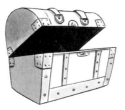

CHAPTER EIGHT

The next day was Saturday, and Rowan and Astrid had promised their parents they would help out in the diner for the breakfast rush. They were anxious to get to the post office and so preoccupied with the treasure hunt that they ended up being no help at all.

"Are you sure this is decaf?" asked Mrs. Rossi as Astrid began to refill her coffee cup. Mrs. Rossi's eye twitched a little as she said, "I don't think this is decaf."

Astrid looked at the coffee pot just in time to notice that it was, indeed, not decaf.

"Sorry," she mumbled and hurried off to find the right coffee pot.

Rowan, who had been assigned to the bakery case, wasn't doing much better.

"I said three orange cranberry scones and three bear claws," Mr. Chen said, handing Rowan back the pink bakery box he had just received. "You gave me six sprinkled donuts."

Rowan muttered his apologies and took the box back from Mr. Chen.

Mr. and Mrs. Vega thought Astrid and Rowan were just tired from adjusting to their back-to-school schedule and decided to let them leave early.

"Why don't you go take a nap or something?" suggested Mr. Vega as he added extra scones and bear claws to Mr. Chen's order to make up for Rowan's mistake.

"Maybe," Rowan called as the pair raced out of the diner before their parents could change their minds.

They met up with Jace and Quinn at the Somerville Post Office, which was packed with customers waiting to mail packages.

"Don't these people have anything better to do on a Saturday?" grumbled Rowan as they waited on the front steps for the crowd to clear. They had all agreed they didn't want anyone to see them get the next clue.

Quinn paced excitedly up and down the post office's front steps. "My dad said he can't remember anyone getting past the grocery store clue on the treasure hunt," she said.

"Really?" Astrid asked as she hopped up and began pacing alongside Quinn. "I was beginning to think that maybe it was just a prank that Mick played on the town."

The pair immediately began speculating about what the treasure may be.

"Maybe he left a bunch of money," Astrid said. "My mom said Mick was the most generous person she's ever met."

"I was thinking it might be gold and jewels in a real treasure chest," Quinn said. "That's why he called it a treasure hunt."

Rowan suddenly hissed, "Shhh! Stop talking about it!"

Quinn and Astrid stopped pacing. Astrid opened her mouth to start a fight with her brother but stopped right away when she saw why Rowan had shushed them.

"Hey, guys, looking for clues?" Dirk asked as he strolled up the post office steps.

Quinn, Astrid, and Rowan mumbled hello. Jace decided he'd try one last time to win over Dirk.

"Hey, Dirk!" he called in his friendliest voice. "How's it going?"

Dirk shot Jace an empty look and turned his back on him. He said to Rowan, "Any luck with the treasure hunt? I'm really good at that stuff. Maybe I can help."

Even though Rowan and Dirk had been friends for a long time, Rowan did not like the way he was treating Jace. He knew it was important for Jace to feel like he fit in with the kids at school. Rowan didn't know how to make them get along. "I don't know," he muttered.

Dirk leaned closer to Rowan and whispered, "Listen, why don't we ditch your kid sister and the other two and find the treasure ourselves? That way we only have to split what we find two ways."

Although he had been trying to speak softly, the others heard every word.

"Hey!" exclaimed Astrid.

Rowan gave Astrid a warning look and said to Dirk, "Thanks, but I think we're going to go it on our own."

"You sure?" Dirk asked with a hint of threat in his voice.

"Yeah," Rowan told him, before adding, "Thanks, though."

Dirk wasn't a person who liked to be told no. His face reddened as he stood up. "Whatever," Dirk snapped. "It sounds stupid anyway."

After Dirk stormed away, Rowan lashed out at his sister. "Way to go, Astrid!"

"Why are you blaming me?" Astrid said. "Dirk is your friend, not mine! You don't see any of my friends from school bugging us to join the treasure hunt or offering to leave us out of the prize."

Quinn stood between the quarreling siblings. "Hey, guys, it looks like the post office has emptied out. Let's go find the next clue."

Tensions were high as they made their way to the wall of post office mailboxes. A quick scan of the numbers on the front found box 1383 on the bottom right-hand side of the wall. Astrid peeked into the tiny window on the box.

"There's something inside!" she squealed.

Their excitement over finding the clue was quickly diminished when they realized that the box was locked and they didn't have a key.

"Now what?" Quinn asked.

The foursome stood looking at each other, not sure what to do next.

His frustration with getting so close and being stumped, coupled with his interaction with Dirk, brought Rowan to his boiling point. He balled his hand into a tight fist and banged it against the post office box.

Quinn, Astrid, and Jace jumped back in surprise. They weren't used to seeing Rowan act like that. When they looked back at the box, they were shocked to see that it had popped open.

"What the heck?" said Rowan. He had been embarrassed by his little outburst but was now thrilled with the outcome.

"How did you do that?" asked Jace.

"I have no idea," admitted Rowan.

Before they could take out what was inside the box, Mr. Reynolds, the postmaster, walked over. "Everything okay over here?" he asked. He noticed the opened box. "Hey, is that Mick's box?"

"Um, yes," Rowan mumbled, concerned they may be in trouble for opening someone else's mailbox.

"How did you get it open?" Mr. Reynolds asked.

They exchanged looks before Astrid piped up. "We just tapped on it, and it popped open. We didn't take anything out."

Mr. Reynolds bent down and inspected the box. The four friends were relieved when Mr. Reynolds chuckled and said, "Well, I'll be! That Mick monkeyed with the lock. He must have set it up so it would come open without a key."

Rowan, Jace, Quinn, and Astrid chuckled nervously. They still weren't sure if they were in trouble or not for opening the box.

Mr. Reynolds smiled, shook his head, and said, "That Mick was quite the character. He prepaid for this post office box for the next twenty years. He said that if anyone ever got it open, they could make a copy of what was inside. I thought he was just joking like he always did, but he made sure I understood: Whoever opened it could make a copy, but whatever was in there needed to be returned to the box."

Mr. Reynolds scratched his head and continued, "It never made any sense, but then again, half of the stuff Mick did was a wonder to me. Were you looking for something?"

Jace explained to Mr. Reynolds how the treasure hunt clues had led them to the post office. Mr. Reynolds's eyes widened. "Oh! I remember that now. How funny to think that all this time a clue had been right under my nose."

When Rowan didn't move, Mr. Reynolds gestured toward the box and said, "Well, go ahead! Get your next clue."

With a trembling hand, Rowan reached in and took out a plain envelope.

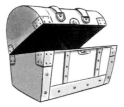

CHAPTER NINE

"What is it?" Astrid demanded as they gathered around Rowan. In her mind, her brother was taking his sweet time revealing their next clue.

Astrid, Jace, and Quinn couldn't keep still as Rowan held the envelope he had removed from Mick's mailbox. Even Mr. Reynolds couldn't wait to see what was inside. He was so excited, in fact, that he moved in for a closer look and blocked out Quinn.

"Ahem," Quinn quietly said, alerting Mr. Reynolds to her presence.

The postmaster immediately backed up to include Quinn and, seeming embarrassed, mumbled, "Sorry."

Whatever patience Astrid had had with her brother was gone. "Open it," she said. Under her breath, she muttered, "And you call me dramatic."

Rowan flipped the envelope over a few times in his hand. It was a generic white envelope with no writing on either side. After he made sure there were no clues on the outside, Rowan ran his finger along the edge, and the envelope popped right open.

He carefully took out a single piece of white paper that had been folded several times in order to fit into the envelope. When Rowan unfolded it, he couldn't believe his eyes.

Quinn, who was still being partially blocked by Mr. Reynolds, stood on her tiptoes and said, "What is it? What does it say?"

With a look of astonishment, Rowan said, "It's a treasure map!"

"It sure is," Mr. Reynolds added. "There's a red X and everything!"

Just then a large crash came from the back of the post office, followed by a yelp from Mrs. Studebaker, the woman who worked at the counter.

Excitement drained from Mr. Reynolds's face, and with a frown he grumbled, "I'd better go see if Arlene is okay. Feel free to use the copy machine before you go. Make sure you put the envelope back like you found it, okay? I promised Mick."

The kids agreed and thanked Mr. Reynolds for his help. As the postmaster headed toward the back room he mumbled, "She's probably nosing around in the packages again."

Jace glanced around the post office to see if anyone had noticed their discovery. He was relieved to find that Dirk was nowhere in sight. "Let's make a copy and get out of here," he said.

There was a copy machine in the post office lobby for patrons to use. Rowan made a copy of both sides of the map and the envelope.

Rowan folded the map and returned it to the envelope. He pressed along the edge to try to reseal it before placing it back in the box, exactly as he'd found it. Secretly he hoped that no one else would ever need to go looking for it. He carefully shut the mailbox, which made a soft clicking sound as it closed. Satisfied with his work, they all made their way quickly out of the post office.

It was agreed that they'd head over to Quinn's house, since it was the closest. It wasn't until they were settled on Quinn's front porch, and certain that no one was around, that they laid out the pieces of paper.

"I can't believe that the next clue is an actual treasure map!" said Astrid, who had already begun fantasizing again about what they may find.

"I know!" Jace agreed. "We're so close! All we need to do is find out where it leads."

Rowan didn't join in their excitement. He frowned as he studied the map. Finally he said, "This map is useless."

"What do you mean?" Quinn asked, pointing to the map. "There's a big X right there. What does it say next to it?"

"Ten paces east of the tallest tree,'" Rowan said glumly. "But there are no trees shown and Somerville must have about a million trees!"

Astrid, Quinn, and Jace leaned over the map to get a better look. At the top of the page in faint, but ornate, lettering, it read: "Somerville, Est. 1860." Below that there was a drawing indicating a mountain range with a big X located a few inches below it. In the bottom right-hand corner was written "Map 199, Turner."

"Well, the mountain is probably Becker Mountain," Jace said, referring to the mountain range that separated Somerville from nearby Watertown.

"Probably," Rowan said. "But without any more information, it's hard to tell how far the X is from the mountains. Without a key of some sort, it could be one mile or ten miles. Plus, it's hard to tell what part of Becker Mountain is shown."

Rowan picked up the paper to examine it more closely. "It looks like a lot of the details have been erased or covered up," he said. He pointed to just above the map number in the bottom corner and added, "It looks like the key used to be here but was covered up. If you look closely you can see faint brushstrokes from correction fluid or paint."

Astrid was frustrated. Her daydreams of spending their treasure were fading. "Why would Mick cover up the key?" she asked. "How are we supposed to find the treasure now?"

Quinn looked again at the map. "Mick did leave us some clues," she said. "There's a map number on the bottom. Maybe we're supposed to find the original map with all the information. If we find that, we can definitely find where this X is located."

Rowan nodded. "That's a great idea. Where can we find old maps?"

Jace studied the map closer. Suddenly his face lit up. "I just remembered something! When we first moved into the Potters' place, I was bored and did a little exploring. I found a map in the attic that looks a lot like this one. We should compare them."

"It's worth a shot," Astrid said and jumped up, happy that they had a plan. "Let's go find ourselves a map!"

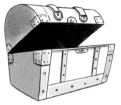

CHAPTER TEN

The second floor of the Potters' place had been renovated as beautifully as the first floor. The wide, cherrywood staircase curved up dramatically from the foyer and led to a long hallway with several doors on each side.

Astrid, Quinn, and Rowan had spent most of their time at the Potters' place on the first floor and couldn't hide their impressed expressions as they reached the top of the stairs.

"This house is fan-cy!" Astrid exclaimed as they walked down the long hallway.

Jace blushed slightly. "Thanks," he said. "It kind of reminds me of a hotel because it's so big and has so many doors. If I want to annoy Evie, I just knock on her door and say 'room service'!"

A burgundy runner ran down the center of the polished wood floors and led to a smaller, less grand staircase. When the foursome made their way to the end of the hallway, it was clear that this was where the renovation had ended.

Jace began the climb up the rickety old staircase to the attic, but Quinn, Astrid, and Rowan were unsure and stood motionless at the bottom. The three of them wore the same looks they'd had the first time they'd walked into the Potters' place. It was as if all the ghost stories and rumors about the old house had come flooding back to them.

Jace was almost to the attic when he realized he was all alone. He turned around and called, "Come on! The map is over here."

When the others didn't move, Jace jogged back down the stairs.

"What's going on?" he asked his friends.

Astrid shrugged and said, "It's kind of creepy, don't you think?"

Quinn glanced up the stairs with a look of uncertainty. "What's even up there?" she asked.

Jace let out a loud laugh. "A bunch of old stuff," he said. "No skeletons or ghosts."

Quinn, Astrid, and Rowan slowly followed Jace up the creaky stairs. About halfway up, Jace stopped and said, "At least I *hope* there aren't any skeletons or ghosts."

Rowan playfully shoved Jace, and they continued their ascent. At the top of the stairs, Jace pulled on a cord that lit a dangling light, barely brightening the stuffy and dusty room.

Quinn crossed her arms across her chest as if she were afraid to touch anything. "I can't believe you came up here by yourself," she said to Jace. "You're crazy."

"That will show you how bored I was before I met you guys," Jace said, which immediately gave him a sick feeling in his stomach. He thought about how no one else at school liked him. He couldn't help but be worried that if Dirk got his way, Rowan, Astrid, and Quinn might change their minds about him, too.

"Let's get the map and get out of here," Astrid said from her spot at the top of the stairs. She hadn't dared to venture any farther into the creepy attic.

There wasn't much in the room except for some boxes and a few pieces of old furniture. Jace moved a few things around before finding what he'd been looking for.

"Here it is!" Jace exclaimed as he held up a large piece of paper. He spread it out underneath the lightbulb so they could get a better look.

The paper was yellowed and brittle and looked a lot like Mick's map. Across the top in similar writing it read "Somerville Expansion." In the bottom right-hand corner was written "Map 232, Turner," with a legend above it. In the lower left-hand corner was a mountain range, and toward the center a large body of water.

"It looks like this map was made around the same time by the same person," Jace said. "Maybe Turner was the mapmaker?"

"Turner—that's Dirk's last name," Quinn noted. "If I remember correctly from the research I did for my project, I think the Turners were some of the original founders of Somerville."

Jace kept his eyes on the map for fear that his friends would see the uncomfortable look on his face at the mention of Dirk's name.

He didn't need to worry, though. Rowan and Quinn were too busy looking at the map.

"See?" Rowan said as he pointed to the legend. "I bet the map we're looking for has the same information on it. With a key to the map, we'll be able to see where the X is located."

Astrid's curiosity got the best of her and she ventured away from the top of the stairs and over to the others.

As soon as she saw the map she said, "Isn't that Watertown?"

The others looked again as Astrid pointed at the mountains in the bottom left-hand corner. "That's Becker Mountain," she said. Then she pointed at the water. "And that's Lake Camille."

After a moment, Quinn nodded her head. "I think that is Watertown! Whoever made this map must have wanted to make it part of Somerville."

As interesting as the map was, it wasn't helping them find the treasure. Rowan turned to Jace. "Where did you find this? Maybe the map we're looking for was with it?"

Jace walked over to a huge, old chest. It was made of light-colored pinewood with dark iron hardware, including a very sturdy-looking lock.

"How did you get in it?" Rowan asked as he lifted the hefty lock.

Jace smiled and said, "I didn't. I tried and tried to open that lock, but couldn't. The map was sticking out a bit so I carefully pulled it out."

Rowan, Quinn, and Astrid knelt down to study the chest. There was a small gap between the base and lid where the map had been poking out.

Rowan turned toward Astrid and said, "You've got tiny fingers. See if you can reach in there and pull something out."

Astrid frowned with annoyance. She didn't like to be told what to do, especially by her brother. Begrudgingly, she poked her finger in the gap and began to run it along the edge. After a few seconds, she yanked her hand back quickly and yelped, "Ouch!"

"Did something bite you?" Quinn asked.

Astrid rubbed her finger and said, "No, but I think I got a splinter."

Rowan didn't have time for Astrid's antics. "Try again and be more careful," he ordered.

Astrid stuck out her tongue at him and carefully poked her finger into the gap. She felt around and then shifted her hand so she could use her thumb, too. Her eyebrows crinkled with concentration. But a moment later, a big smile crossed her face as she pulled something out from the crack. "I've got something!" she exclaimed. She carefully pinched and pulled until it was free.

Upon further investigation, they saw that Astrid had retrieved an old photograph from the chest. It was a bit blurry and faded, but in it stood two men with somber faces. Below them was written "Abel Potter and Jeremiah Turner, ready to expand Somerville."

At first glance, it wasn't a very interesting photograph. Nor was it that shocking to find it in the attic of the Potters' place. When they looked closer, though, the four of them grew more excited.

"It's him!" Quinn exclaimed.

"It is!" Astrid said. "It's the same guy from the museum picture!"

At the end of the summer, the foursome had stumbled upon what they'd thought would be their next mystery. In the town's tiny museum they'd found a picture of Somerville's founders, which included a man with the last name Potter.

The man responsible for bringing Jace and Evie to Somerville was a secret agent who went by the name Mr. P. They were shocked to find that the man labeled as Potter in the old picture looked exactly like Mr. P., a quirky man they knew little about.

The foursome had scoured the museum for more clues but came up short. They did their best to get information out of Mr. P., who would neither confirm nor deny their suspicions and would only say, "No comment."

Rowan smiled. "And in this picture he looks even more like Mr. P.! Seems like we've got two mysteries to solve now!"

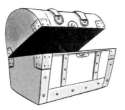

CHAPTER ELEVEN

Astrid, Quinn, Rowan, and Jace knew from the last time they'd questioned Mr. P. that he wasn't going to give them any direct answers about his family history. When the foursome had originally asked him about the picture they'd seen in the Somerville Museum, he had given them absolutely no information. For a seasoned secret agent, questions from four kids under the age of thirteen had been no problem. Within seconds he had them so confused that, for a moment, they couldn't even remember why they were questioning him in the first place. Before they could regain their composure, he'd promptly ended the conversation. "We're finished here," he'd said and hung up the phone.

If they were going to approach Mr. P. again about being a Potter, they wanted to have supporting evidence and a solid game plan. They needed to learn more about Abel Potter, Mr. P.'s look-alike, so they headed to the Somerville Library to do some research.

As they passed the information desk, Mrs. Sager, the librarian, greeted them warmly. "Hello, kids! Looking for more clues today?"

"You could say that," Astrid replied mysteriously as they walked by.

"Good luck!" Mrs. Sager called behind them.

Quinn directed them to where the books on local history were shelved. She had spent plenty of time there lately doing research for her paper on her family's history.

"I think we need to start with the founding of Watertown," Rowan said as they headed toward the back of the library.

"I agree," said Quinn. "The map that we found definitely looked a lot like Watertown, but it was labeled 'Somerville Expansion.'"

"And the picture of Abel Potter, aka Mr. P.'s twin, said something about expanding Somerville," Astrid added.

"What I don't understand is this: Why is it called Watertown if it was meant to be a part of Somerville?" Jace asked.

"Good question," Rowan said. "Let's find out."

A quick search of the library's catalog on the computer produced a few books about the history of Watertown. They each grabbed one from the shelf and gathered around a large wooden table. They quietly paged through the books in hopes of finding something about Abel Potter.

"Listen to this," Rowan whispered when he stumbled upon something interesting. They all stopped looking through their books to listen. "It says, 'Unlike the founding of the nearby towns Somerville and Westerville, the original history of Watertown has, for the most part, been a mystery to historians.'"

"Oh, great. If the historians can't figure out this mystery, how can we?" Astrid said.

Quinn and Jace chuckled, but Rowan frowned at his sister before continuing. "'It is believed that Watertown was founded by a small group of people, possibly a family, who did not keep records of the town's early days. So little information has been found, in fact, that it almost appears to have been hidden on purpose.'"

"Someone must have gotten to Watertown before the Potters and the Turners," Jace said.

Quinn nodded. "That explains why it's called Watertown instead of being a part of Somerville."

"Maybe," Rowan said, discouraged that they had hit a dead end again in their hunt for information about Abel Potter.

Rowan scanned his book some more before shutting it in frustration. He was about to go get another book when he saw the look on Astrid's face change from boredom to excitement.

"You guys! Look at this!" she said, pointing to the book in front of her. Astrid had grown tired of reading about Watertown. Instead she had been flipping through the books and looking at pictures.

Quinn and Rowan came around from the other side of the table and stood behind her. Jace leaned over from his seat to get a better look. There, underneath Astrid's finger, was a grainy black-and-white picture of a man with the same hooked nose and small chin of Mr. P. Underneath the picture it read, "Alistair Porterfield, believed to be the founder of Watertown."

Rowan leaned over his sister and looked closer. There was no mistaking the similarities. "That sure looks like Abel Potter to me," he said.

"Is there any other information?" Quinn asked, gazing over Jace's shoulder.

Astrid quickly scanned the page. For the most part it confirmed what Rowan had already read: the history of Watertown was a mystery for the first twenty years or so, and the town was believed to have been founded by a small group of secretive, unnamed people.

"So, Potter changed his name and moved to Watertown?" Rowan asked. "I guess that explains where the Potters went when they disappeared from Somerville."

"Everyone says that no one liked them. I'm not surprised they moved out and kept it a secret," Astrid added.

"Maybe that means the 'P' in Mr. P. actually stands for 'Porterfield,'" Quinn said, thrilled with the fact that they'd finally found some information.

She turned to look at Jace and found him white as a ghost, with a stunned expression on his face. "What's wrong?" she asked.

Before he could stop himself, Jace blurted out, "My last name is Porterfield."

Astrid gave him a funny look. "No, it's not, silly!" she said. "Your last name is Carson."

Rowan looked at his sister with supreme annoyance. "He's undercover, remember?" he said. "He's never told us his real name."

"Oh!" Astrid said. "I forgot!"

It all made sense to her. She looked at Jace and whispered what they all were thinking. "Jace . . . that means . . . you might be a Potter."

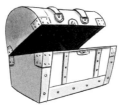

CHAPTER TWELVE

Jace stayed home the rest of the weekend and let the calls from his friends go unanswered. He couldn't wrap his brain around what they'd seen at the library. There was no mistaking that the picture of Alistair Porterfield looked exactly like the ones of Abel Potter, and that those looked eerily similar to the man he knew as Mr. P.

But if he and Mr. P. were related, wouldn't Jace already know that? He tried to think of what he knew about Mr. P., which wasn't much. Jace hadn't even met Mr. P. until his parents found themselves in trouble about a year before. Since that time, Mr. P. had acted almost like a parent to Jace and his sister, Evie, and let them rely on him for everything. He had gone above and beyond to make sure Jace and Evie were safe and comfortable. Was he doing that because he was good at his job? Or was it because they were related? The thought had never crossed Jace's mind.

Jace knew very little about his family history. He understood that was the way it had to be because both of his parents were secret agents. They had changed their location and identities more times than Jace could count. He hadn't even thought of the name Porterfield for years. His parents had always said that one day they would settle down and be a typical family. Jace had never minded their lifestyle before, but for the first time he'd begun to think of somewhere as home, and he wanted his parents to settle down in Somerville with him.

He'd had high hopes that it would actually happen until he learned he might be a member of the most hated family in the small town's history. It was bad enough that the kids in school already didn't like him, but now the rest of the town might despise him as well. The thought of leaving his new friends, and a town he had grown to like, made him feel awful.

At school on Monday, Jace found Rowan waiting for him at his locker when he arrived.

"What's up?" Rowan asked. He leaned against the locker next to Jace's, trying his best to act as if everything was normal.

"Hey," Jace responded as he opened up his locker, avoiding eye contact with Rowan.

"What'd you do all weekend?" Rowan asked.

"Not much," Jace mumbled into his locker.

"You missed it," Rowan said. "Miss Coco tried to convince Mayor Arnold that you can't hum while holding your nose."

"You can't?" Jace looked up with interest. He couldn't resist a good Miss Coco story.

Rowan continued, "That's what Miss Coco told us. Before long she had Mayor Arnold, and everyone in the diner, holding their noses and trying to hum. When my mom walked out from the kitchen, she thought everyone had gone crazy. It was hilarious!"

Jace laughed out loud. He could picture the scene in his mind. Thinking of Mick's Diner and the friendly people of Somerville made him sad, though. Sometimes he felt like he really belonged in Somerville, and other times he felt like an outsider.

Rowan saw the smile fade from Jace's face. He knew Jace was thinking about what they'd found at the library. He leaned closer and said, "I was thinking maybe we should drop the Mr. P. mystery. Besides, even if it's true, you know it's no big deal, right? Nobody even talks about the Potters anymore."

Jace felt overwhelmed and confused. He slammed his locker shut and looked around to make sure no one was listening.

"I'd better go," he said without looking up. "I'll see you in class."

Rowan felt helpless as he watched his friend walk alone down the hallway. He didn't understand why Dirk, and therefore Dirk's friends, were treating Jace so awfully.

As if reading his mind, Dirk appeared out of nowhere. He punched Rowan on the arm a little harder than Rowan liked and said, "Hey, Rowan! How's it going?"

"Okay," Rowan said as he rubbed his now-sore arm. He paused a moment and then added, "Hey, what's your deal with Jace? Why don't you like him?"

Dirk considered the question before answering. "I don't know," he said flatly. "I just don't."

"He's a really cool guy," Rowan said. "You should get to know him."

Dirk looked unconvinced. "Nah. I don't like him. Plus, he lives in that creepy old house. It's weird."

Rowan was frustrated. Not only did Dirk dislike Jace, he didn't even have a good reason. Before

Rowan could say anything else to change his mind, Dirk changed the subject. "So, when are you going to let me help with the treasure hunt? I know I could find that treasure!"

Rowan was still thinking about how to get Dirk to like Jace and replied absentmindedly, "We're good, but thanks."

Dirk, who had asked Rowan several times now, finally lost what little patience he'd had to begin with. "Listen, I don't know why you'd rather hang out with that kid and your little sister, but I want in on that treasure hunt. If you don't ditch them and work with me, I'll find other people to hunt with."

Rowan was stunned. There was no way he was dropping the others, but how could he keep Dirk from looking for the treasure as well?

When Rowan didn't respond, Dirk said, "Fine. Good luck beating me to that treasure."

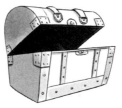

CHAPTER THIRTEEN

When Mr. P. had relocated Jace and Evie to Somerville, he'd instructed both of them to come up with what he called "an emergency word." It needed to be something they could easily remember during a crisis situation. The emergency word was to be used only if they found themselves in a life-or-death situation, as it would notify Mr. P. to the level of danger they were facing. All Jace and Evie had to do was call Mr. P. and say the word and he would be there immediately, no questions asked.

Jace had chosen the word "tiger," his favorite animal, and, so far, he had never had to use it. With the discovery that he may be a Potter descendant, he found himself in a situation that, while not life-or-death, was urgent nonetheless.

He called Mr. P. and, in all seriousness, uttered one word: "Kitten."

Mr. P. was silent for a moment before replying, "Excuse me?"

"Kitten," Jace said again. "I'm in a situation that's not quite 'tiger' status, but it's important."

Mr. P. made a small noise that was about as close as he came to laughing and said, "I'll be there in an hour."

Exactly 60 minutes later, there was a knock on the door of the Potters' place.

Mr. P. wasn't one for pleasantries. Without so much as a hello, he walked through the door, past Jace, and into the living room. After he was seated on the couch, he looked Jace directly in the eye and said, "Well?"

Jace was used to Mr. P.'s abruptness, but still he was nervous. Part of him wanted to know the truth, and the other part wanted to pretend that nothing had happened.

"So, um, well," Jace stammered as he sunk down into a chair across from Mr. P. "It's just that . . ."

Mr. P. sighed. "Jace, what is it?"

Jace looked closely at Mr. P. He studied the man's face, looking for similarities to his own. Mr. P. almost always wore dark sunglasses, even indoors, but he had taken them off as he'd walked in. For the first time, Jace noticed that Mr. P.'s eyes were the exact same shape and pale shade of green as his own, a trait he'd inherited from his mother. How had he failed to notice that before?

Mr. P. looked impatient. While Jace was still trying to figure out how to ask all the questions he wanted answered, Mr. P. said, "Your parents are coming home."

Jace was stunned. For a moment he forgot all about the Potter nonsense and was filled with happiness. "They are? When? That's so great!"

A tiny smile flashed across Mr. P.'s face before he immediately went back to his serious expression. "In a few weeks," he said. "The agency is certain that your whole family is out of danger. They are most grateful to all of you for the sacrifices you've made. Both of your parents will be retiring after this mission. You should be very proud. Your parents have had long, successful careers with the agency."

Jace had looked forward to the day his parents would retire and they could all be together. Combined with the drama that was already going on, the news felt overwhelming. "What happens now?" he asked.

Mr. P. sat back on the couch. "Well, that's something we need to discuss. I've talked to Evie, and she would like to stay here in Somerville. It seems she has become quite taken with a Mr. Marcus Sloane."

Jace was surprised, although he normally paid

no attention to Evie's social life. "Marcus from Earl's Gas Station?"

Mr. P. nodded. "Apparently, they've gotten to know each other quite well." Mr. P. shifted in his seat, looking a bit uncomfortable. "She spoke with me about it a while ago and said she wanted to make the relationship a, um, romantic one."

Jace smiled. He had never seen Mr. P. look even remotely uncomfortable. He found it funny that romance was the subject that could shake his normally cool demeanor.

Mr. P. returned to his stoic self and went on. "We've done a thorough check on Mr. Sloane and his immediate family, and he has been cleared. I've spoken with him myself. He has been given the information he needs to know—mainly that you and Evie are siblings and your parents are secret agents—and little else. He has been sworn to secrecy, although at this point we feel very confident that the risk to your family has been eliminated and their identities no longer need protecting."

Jace nodded slowly as he took it all in. His sister was in love with Marcus Sloane, and his parents were coming home for good. He couldn't believe how drastically his life had changed in a few minutes.

He managed to say, "Wow."

Mr. P. continued. "I have spoken with your parents, and they are both thrilled that you and your sister have enjoyed your time here. In fact, they both rather liked the idea of living here in a small town but wanted to leave it up to you. Is it safe to assume from our previous conversations that you would like to stay indefinitely in Somerville?"

A week ago this would have been very easy for Jace to answer. With his questions for Mr. P. still left unanswered, he didn't know how he wanted to respond. Jace knew that it was now or never if he wanted to find out the truth about being a Potter.

He took a deep breath and said, "There are a few things I need to know first."

CHAPTER FOURTEEN

Once Jace started talking, he found it difficult to stop. The events of the past few weeks—the treasure hunt and stumbling upon the map and photograph—poured out of him in an almost frantic way. When he finished, Jace felt drained and a little bit relieved.

Mr. P. kept silent, staring at the floor. He had shown no emotion while Jace was speaking and hadn't given any indication as to what he might say. If he was surprised by Jace's findings, there was no way of knowing.

Jace wasn't sure what to do, so he started talking again. "I know the last time we asked you about being a Potter, you wouldn't tell us. That's fine. But now it's about *me* being a Potter, and it's really important for me to know."

"You are a Potter," Mr. P. said, stopping Jace before he could start rambling again. He looked Jace directly in the eyes and said again, "You are a Potter."

Even though he'd thought this might be the case, Jace didn't know how to react to the news. He looked blankly at Mr. P., and before he could ask his next question, Mr. P. answered it. "I'm a Potter, too."

Now Jace was speechless. He was glad when Mr. P. spoke again. "Where did you find this map and picture?" he asked.

Jace pointed up and said, "In the attic."

Mr. P. nodded. He got up and disappeared into the kitchen. When he returned he was holding an antique-looking key. He said to Jace, "Come on, there are some things up there that will explain everything."

Jace stood on wobbly legs and followed Mr. P. up the stairs to the second floor and then up the back staircase to the attic. Mr. P. was moving more quickly. By the time Jace made it to the attic, he found Mr. P. kneeling next to the open trunk and sorting through its contents. Once he found the items he was looking for, Mr. P. sat down on the floor and indicated for Jace to do the same. Jace moved slowly across the room and joined him.

"I guess there is no better place to start than at the beginning," Mr. P. said with a sigh. "The settling of Somerville started before the founders even began their trek west. Each family that was asked to join the journey was invited because of a talent or skill they could bring to the new town. Abel Potter, his wife, Camille, and their four sons were asked to come along because the Potters were highly skilled builders. In fact, Abel and his sons built almost every one of the original buildings and houses in Somerville."

Jace looked up with surprise and asked, "Really?"

Mr. P. nodded. "Yes. Abel was an innovative builder and was always looking for the best way to construct things. He tried out new techniques and materials on his own house before using them on others. That's why this house looks a little peculiar on the outside."

Jace chuckled, remembering how his friends thought the old house was haunted.

"When the crew came to remodel this house, they were shocked by how well it had held up. They said they had never seen such solid craftsmanship," Mr. P. added.

Jace felt a twinge of pride at the thought of being a Potter.

Mr. P. continued, "Abel worked closely with a man named Jeremiah Turner, who was a cartographer, and the pair became great friends."

"A cart-what-a-pher?" Jace asked.

"A cartographer," Mr. P. said again. "It's another way to say 'mapmaker.'"

"That's why his name is on the maps," Jace said. Thinking of the name Turner made him think of Dirk. In a softer voice, Jace added, "I think the Turners still live in Somerville."

"I wouldn't doubt it," Mr. P. said. "Turner and Potter were critical in the settling of Somerville. As people bought their property, Turner would draw up a map, and Potter would build the house. Dividing up the property was an important part of the town's founding, and the settlers were grateful for the hard work the Potters did."

Jace interrupted Mr. P. "Wait. Are you saying that people *liked* the Potters?"

Mr. P. nodded and looked through his stack of items from the trunk. "Oh, yes. They worked hard and for a fair wage and made Somerville feel like a real town in a matter of years."

Mr. P. found what he was looking for and laid an old newspaper on the floor. On the front page was the headline "Potter Named Citizen of the Year." Jace scanned the article quickly and read how Abel and his sons were being honored by the town for all they had done. The article was full of quotes from different townspeople expressing their gratitude.

Jace looked at Mr. P. with confusion. "But I thought everyone hated the Potters?"

"Well, that story came later and wasn't necessarily true," Mr. P. said with a frown. "After it had been settled and was growing into a booming town, Potter went exploring to find a way to expand Somerville. He and Turner made the difficult trip past Becker Mountain and discovered what is now known as Watertown."

Jace nodded as Mr. P. held up the map that he had already seen.

"According to Abel Potter's journal," said Mr. P. as he held up a thick leather-bound book, "the pair planned to present the expansion to the people of Somerville, but that never happened."

"Why?" Jace asked.

"Potter discovered that Turner had been cheating people by making phony maps and overcharging them for land. He then kept the money for himself. He told Turner that he needed to make right his offenses or he was going to report him to the authorities.

"Turner tried to deny it, but Potter had too much evidence against him. Turner began threatening Potter and his family and started spreading evil rumors about them. He was desperate to shut Potter up and would stop at nothing."

Jace's eyes were wide as he listened to the story. "So, what happened?"

Mr. P. went on. "Potter feared for his family's safety, so he made plans to move them to Watertown and begin again in secrecy. As the Potters prepared for their move, Turner grew more paranoid about the evidence that the family had about him. One night, he snuck to the Potters' place in the middle of the night and tried to set the house on fire. Thankfully, the townspeople rushed to put out the fire and no one was hurt, but Potter immediately moved his family to Watertown and never came back to Somerville. He was devastated to leave the town he loved, but he was more concerned with his family's safety. They changed their last name to Porterfield and started over, very successfully as it turned out.

"When the town realized the Potters had mysteriously disappeared, more people bought into Turner's lies and new rumors were started," Mr. P. explained. "I'm guessing that some of those stories are the same old tales you heard when you first moved here."

Jace nodded. "It makes me mad to know that the Potters were good people, and Turner was the jerk."

"From what I understand, Jeremiah Turner was the only bad apple in the bunch. Since then, the Turners have been upstanding citizens," Mr. P. said.

Jace smirked, thinking about Dirk Turner. He didn't consider Dirk to be an upstanding citizen.

Mr. P. sighed again and said, "And I guess you're wondering how we're related?"

Jace nodded. He had been so intrigued by Mr. P.'s story, he'd almost forgotten about that.

"I am your uncle. Your mother is my baby sister," Mr. P. explained.

"Why did that have to be kept a secret, and why hadn't we met before my parents got into trouble?" Jace asked.

"Your mother is several years younger than me. By the time she had you, I was already deep into the NIA. For years, she and I only saw each other on missions. With some of the things we were working on, it was safer that way," Mr. P. said. "When she and your dad got in trouble, I came out of hiding and volunteered to take care of you and Evie."

Jace smiled at that thought. "Thank you," he said sincerely.

Not one for emotion, Mr. P. began placing the items back into the trunk and without looking at Jace said, "You are most welcome."

When the trunk was repacked, Mr. P. turned toward Jace. "So, do you still want to live in Somerville? No one has to know that you are a Potter. It's ancient history."

Jace felt better knowing that his family members were not the scary misfits they were believed to be, but he still wasn't sure how he felt about staying in a town where people already didn't like him. He knew he could tell everyone about Jeremiah Turner, but what good would that do? Did he want everyone to turn against Dirk? Jace began to worry he'd never find a place to call home.

"Can I think about it?" Jace asked.

"Of course," Mr. P. said as he made his way out of the attic. "But don't take too long."

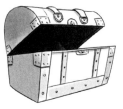

CHAPTER FIFTEEN

Jace didn't go to school the day after he'd met with Mr. P., or the day after that. By the third day, his friends were really worried about him. They went immediately to see Evie at the diner after school.

"Is he sick or something?" Quinn questioned.

"Is it okay if we go see him?" Astrid asked.

"He's not answering the phone and hasn't returned any of our calls," Rowan added.

Evie looked uncomfortable as they peppered her with questions. "I don't know," she said, trying hard to look busy as she restocked the donut display.

Marcus Sloane came into the diner and sat at the counter. With a huge smile on her face, Evie said, "Sorry, guys, I've got a customer. I'll tell Jace you asked about him."

In a flash she made her way over to Marcus.

Rowan, Astrid, and Quinn went back to worrying about their friend. Mrs. Vega walked over to the sad trio and asked, "Why don't you join Dirk and the others on the treasure hunt? I think it's great that you've gotten your friends involved."

Rowan's head snapped up. "Dirk? What are you talking about?"

Mrs. Vega seemed surprised by her son's reaction. "I thought you told the kids at school about your hunt?" she asked. "Dirk and some others were in here right after school a couple of days ago looking for the first clue. They didn't say, but I just assumed you knew about it. They had no idea what the clue meant, so I suggested they try the library."

Rowan frowned and turned toward Astrid and Quinn. "I was afraid this might happen. Let's go see how far they've gotten."

"Is everything okay?" asked Mrs. Vega when she saw the looks on their faces.

"We'll see," Astrid replied grimly.

"I'll explain later," Rowan called as they dashed out of the diner.

By the time they got to the library, they were out of breath from running the entire way.

"Dirk . . . treasure hunt . . . book . . ." Astrid panted as she spoke to a confused Mrs. Sager.

Quinn, who had taken a moment to catch her breath, asked, "Has Dirk Turner been in here looking for a clue in the treasure hunt?"

A smile replaced the confused look on Mrs. Sager's face. "Why, yes! They were in here the other day," she said. "I think it's so great how you've gotten all the kids involved in your little treasure hunt."

Rowan tried his hardest not to lose his cool. "Did they get the next clue?" he asked as calmly as he could manage.

"They did! They had no idea what they were doing, but I helped," Mrs. Sager said, looking very proud of herself. When she saw their frustration, she quickly added, "I didn't give them the answer, just some hints. They figured it out from there."

They thanked Mrs. Sager and headed directly to Goodwin's Market. Mrs. Goodwin greeted them as they raced in.

"Looking for more clues?" she asked with a chuckle. "Some of your friends were in here the other day."

"Did you help them find the clues?" Rowan asked her.

"Nope," Mrs. Goodwin replied. For a split-second Astrid, Quinn, and Rowan were overcome with relief, but then she added, "But Mr. Goodwin did."

"He did?" Astrid whined, slumping her shoulders in disappointment.

"Isn't that okay?" Mrs. Goodwin asked. "I know they should have figured it out themselves, but the store was busy, and he didn't have much time. Plus, he said he didn't want them spending all day crawling under the fruit displays, so he showed them which ones had clues."

"It's okay," Rowan said, but from the sullen look on his face, Mrs. Goodwin surely knew it was not okay.

Astrid, Rowan, and Quinn did not run to the post office. They had a good idea what to expect when they got there and were in no rush. What they didn't expect to see, however, was Dirk and his friends walking out of the post office as they approached.

"Hello there, fellow treasure hunters!" Dirk called, waving a piece of paper in the air. As they got closer, they could see that it was a copy of the map from the mailbox.

"Did someone tell you how to get that clue, like the rest of them?" Astrid said, unable to hide her annoyance.

"Mr. Reynolds was happy to help us," Dirk said smugly. He turned to Rowan. "Ready to join forces and find this treasure?"

"Where are you going to look?" Rowan asked.

Dirk squirmed. "Well, we're not sure yet. But I think we'll figure it out."

Quinn rolled her eyes. "Just like you figured out all of the rest of the clues?" she said.

"Whatever," Dirk said. He turned to his group of friends. "C'mon, let's go find us some treasure!"

Rowan tried not to panic. As they watched Dirk and his friends walk away, he said, "We need Jace."

They went back to running, and by the time they made it to the front door of the Potters' place, they were out of breath again. When Jace answered the door, the three of them began talking over each other.

"Dirk . . . found all the . . . clues," Quinn said between pants.

"He's . . . going to get . . . the treasure," Astrid added, gasping for air.

"We need . . . your help," Rowan said, putting his hands on his knees to catch his breath.

Jace smiled and said, "I think I know where to find the original map."

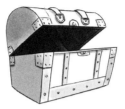

CHAPTER SIXTEEN

As they made their way to the Somerville Museum, Quinn asked Jace how he'd thought to look there.

"Oh, you know," Jace said vaguely. "It just sort of came to me."

Jace was not ready to tell his friends about his visit from Mr. P., or about the decision he had to make. Because of this, he chose not to tell them Mr. P.'s parting words: "Have you looked at the museum? It has quite a collection of maps."

As Rowan, Astrid, and Quinn told him about Dirk and the treasure hunt, Jace realized how much he had missed them. He'd avoided them for days, but they knew about his possible family history, and yet they still treated him the same. Jace began to wonder why he had ever doubted his friends.

When they reached the museum, Mrs. Partridge, the museum's curator, didn't seem surprised to see them at all. Many students had been in lately researching their family histories for school projects, and she was happy to help.

"Hello there!" she said cheerfully. "What can I help you find?"

They showed her the map, and she took them directly to a large binder that said "Turner Maps" on the cover. The maps were stored behind protective plastic covers and organized in numerical order.

The foursome couldn't believe their luck as they flipped the pages and quickly found Map 199. Rowan carefully unfolded the map they had copied from the post office, and Astrid gasped when she realized it was the same as the one in the binder, but the library's version had much more detail.

Quinn pointed to a river that was on the original map but not on their copy. "Isn't that Willow Creek?"

"It must be! There's no other water by the mountains." Rowan was feeling hopeful again. He pointed above the river and said, "This must be Perkin's Outlook. From the key it looks like the X is just south of there."

For a moment, they stood in stunned silence. Could they really be this close to finding the treasure?

"What are we waiting for?" Astrid said finally. "Let's get our bikes and head up there!"

"Now that we know where to look, finding the tallest tree should be easy," Jace added.

They thanked Mrs. Partridge, who was showing a tourist the letter written by Abraham Lincoln. She smiled and waved as they hurried out.

They rode to the area below Perkin's Outlook in silence, each of them too excited to speak. Quinn had grabbed a couple of her mom's gardening hand shovels and now had them in her backpack. The friends were ready to unearth their treasure.

With their bikes stashed behind a large boulder, they made their way on foot toward Willow Creek. None of them had every taken this route to the creek. Most people stayed near a small park located a few miles down the road. As they got closer to the water, they were startled as ancient-looking headstones began to appear.

"What is this place?" Astrid asked, more than a little uncertain about going forward.

"It looks like a cemetery," Quinn said. She bent over to read a crumbling headstone. "'Fido, Beloved Companion, 1921–1930.'"

Rowan walked over to another headstone and read, "'Buddy, World's Greatest Dog, 1934–1941.'"

Jace couldn't believe what he was hearing. "You mean we're walking through a pet cemetery?"

They all looked down to see if they were standing on a grave site. Astrid was, and she flinched, jumping to the right. Everyone felt creeped out.

Quinn tried to put a positive spin on it, saying, "I guess it's sweet that they loved their pets so much."

"Is that an open grave?" Jace asked, pointing to a large hole in the ground a few feet ahead of them.

"If it is, it's huge! Maybe someone was going to bury their pet horse," Astrid said, shivering at the thought.

Rowan didn't want to hang around among the decaying headstones and unfilled graves. "Let's get out of here," he said.

As they began to press on, they heard a loud crack come from behind them. They all spun around to see what had made the noise.

"What the heck?" Astrid said, crouched down in fear that a ghost dog or spirit cat had risen up from the grave.

There was silence for a moment before the friends heard voices. They were as soft as whispers, but it was clear they were coming from behind them.

"Hello?" Rowan shouted. "We know you're there! Come out!"

"Come out?" Astrid hissed. "Why are you inviting the ghosts to come out?"

Rowan shook his head in annoyance. After another moment, a group of kids emerged from the trees. Someone had been following them, and it was none other than Dirk and his friends.

As they approached, Rowan asked, "How did you figure out the clue?"

"We didn't," boasted Marty, a boy in the same grade as Jace and Rowan. "We saw you coming out of the museum and tailed you."

Dirk punched Marty in the arm, obviously mad at him for exposing their dirty methods. He turned toward Rowan and said, "It doesn't matter how we got here. We just want to know where to find the treasure."

"No way," Rowan said sternly. He waved the map in his hand. "We found this map on our own, and the treasure belongs to us."

Dirk lurched toward Rowan to grab the map. In his haste, he hadn't noticed the giant hole in the ground between him and Rowan. He tried to stop himself, but it was too late, and he fell forward toward the deep and disgusting pit below. In the nick of time, Jace lunged forward and grabbed the back of Dirk's shirt and pulled him to safety.

Dirk was in shock as he spun around toward Jace. When he saw who had saved him, Dirk was stunned. Why would someone he had treated so poorly risk getting hurt to save him? Dirk looked down at the ground and said, "Thanks."

Jace was surprised by Dirk's sincerity. With a shrug he replied, "No problem."

Dirk looked around at all the headstones and asked, "What is this place?"

Rowan chuckled. "Didn't you read the headstones? It's an abandoned pet cemetery."

Dirk shuddered, his face puckered as if he'd just eaten something gross. He turned and spoke directly to Jace. "Look, this is getting out of control. We don't want to fight. We know you guys did all the work on the treasure hunt. All we wanted was to join the fun. Can we at least go with you to find the treasure? Whatever it is, it's all yours."

While still annoyed by how Dirk had treated him, Jace realized what he really wanted was to forget it and move on. He looked at Quinn, Astrid, and Rowan for their input. The three of them were smiling, clearly happy that the drama with Dirk apparently had been put behind them.

"It's up to you," Rowan told him.

"Whatever you think," Astrid added.

Jace smiled, feeling grateful for his friends.

"Let's go," Jace said to Dirk.

Everyone followed Rowan, carefully dodging around the headstones. When they made it to the river, the tallest tree was easy to spot. The mood was festive as they loudly counted off the ten paces to the east. Taking turns, they dug using Quinn's hand shovels. At last, Jace hit upon something hard. Everyone began digging with their bare hands. Slowly but surely they unearthed a wooden box the size of a carton of eggs.

"It feels light," Rowan said.

Tired and happy but exhausted, they all stared at the box for a moment. Rowan wiped dirt off to reveal an engraving on the top:

This box may be plain and an ordinary size
But I assure you, my friend, inside is a prize!
I hope you'll enjoy and regale with delight
And think of dear Mick with every bite!

Everyone held their breath as Rowan slowly opened the treasure box. Inside was a folded piece of white paper.

"Is it another clue?" Jace asked.

Rowan unfolded the paper and read what was written on it. After a moment he replied, "Nope. It's the treasure."

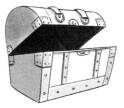

CHAPTER SEVENTEEN

News of the discovery of Mick's treasure spread quickly through Somerville, and a celebration was organized right away. Mick's Diner was the perfect place for such an event, and nearly the whole town came out for it.

Astrid, Rowan, Quinn, and Jace sat at a table toward the back of the diner, the only ones not having a great time.

"I still can't believe the treasure was Mick's cherry pie recipe," Astrid said, dropping her fork noisily onto her plate.

Jace scooped a huge bite of pie into his mouth and, with a cherry-covered smile, said, "I know, but this pie is amazing!"

When Rowan had told the group that the treasure was Mick's legendary cherry pie recipe, they realized instantly that they had been the victims in one of Mick's infamous pranks.

The rest of the town had been absolutely thrilled with the discovery. Nobody was happier than Mr. and Mrs. Vega. Mrs. Vega followed her old friend's recipe exactly, and tears came to her eyes when she tasted the first bite. The pie was perfect, and her best memories of Mick came rushing back.

As the foursome ate their pie in frustrated silence, Dirk and a couple of kids from school made their way over.

"I know it's not gold and jewels, but that pie is really good," Dirk said with a laugh.

They all nodded and murmured their agreement.

Dirk leaned over and said quietly to Jace, "Hey, I just wanted to say I'm sorry for being such a jerk to you before and thank you again for saving me from falling into that hole. If I had twisted my ankle or broken something, my basketball season would have been ruined!"

"It was nothing," Jace replied.

A look crossed Dirk's face as if he'd just had a great idea. "You're tall," he said to Jace. "Do you play basketball?"

Jace nodded and said, "A little."

"You should totally try out for the team!" Dirk said with excitement. "We need a big guy in the middle. It'll be a total blast!"

"Maybe," Jace said with a shrug. He'd never stayed in one place long enough to be a part of a team, but the thought made him very happy.

Dirk stood back up and said to everyone, "We're heading over to the bowling alley. Do you guys want to come with?"

Rowan glanced at the other three, who nodded in agreement. "Sounds good," he told Dirk.

As they stood to leave, Jace said, "We'll catch up with you guys. There's something we need to do first."

Rowan, Astrid, and Quinn looked confused but sat back down.

"See you there," Dirk said, leading his friends toward the door.

"What's up?" Rowan asked. "Don't you want to hang out with Dirk and those guys?"

"Yes, it sounds fun," Jace replied. "There's just some stuff I need to tell you."

On the day they had found the treasure, Jace knew for certain that he really did want to stay in Somerville. It was his home now, and thanks to his best friends, he knew he belonged.

Jace told the others about what he had learned from Mr. P. about the Potter/Porterfield family. Their eyes were wide as he told the story. He did not refer to Jeremiah Turner by name. He had decided before beginning his story that there was no need to create any drama between himself and Dirk, and that exposing the Turners' history was unnecessary.

"You mean you are related to that robot, Mr. P.?" Astrid asked.

Jace laughed. "Yep. I guess he's my Uncle Robot."

"We should tell people the truth about the Potters," Rowan decided.

"It's ancient history," Jace said, shaking his head to dismiss the idea. He and his friends knew the truth about his family's history, and that was all that mattered.

Rowan stood up to go. "Let's go bowl!"

"There's more," Jace said.

"More?" Rowan asked as he sat back down.

"My parents are safe from any danger and are retiring from the agency," Jace began. "They are coming home. We can finally settle down and live a normal life."

Quinn, Astrid, and Rowan were happy for Jace but unsure what it meant.

"So . . . does this mean you'll be moving away?" Quinn asked nervously.

"Nope," Jace said, beaming. "We get to stay in Somerville!"

They couldn't contain their happiness. A giant cheer erupted from their table. People around them assumed they were enjoying the pie and paid no attention.

Mr. Vega appeared and passed out more pie to everyone. "Looks like you guys finally decided to celebrate after all!"

"We sure did!" Astrid said, giving a knowing look to the others. They had plenty to be happy about.

Rowan raised his fork and said, "Here's to us!"

They clinked their forks, and Jace added, "And here's to all the mysteries we'll solve together!"

About the Author

Raised in the Chicago suburb of Hoffman Estates, Michele Jakubowski has the teachers in her life to thank for her love of reading and writing. While writing has always been a passion for Michele, she believes it is the books she has read throughout the years, and the teachers who assigned them, that have made her the storyteller she is today. Michele lives in Powell, Ohio, with her husband, John, and their children, Jack and Mia.

Discussion

1. Mick left clues around town at the library, post office, and grocery store. How do you think he was able to leave them without anyone noticing? Brainstorm and come up with your own ideas on how Mick was able to leave his treasure hunt hints.

2. Secrets play a big role in the story. Who do you think had the biggest secret? Was it Mick's clues? Jace and Evie's secret identities? Mr. P.'s family history? Support your opinion with examples from the story.

3. Mick went on vacation but never returned to Somerville. After reading the story about his pranks, do you think Mick really died? Or could he still be out there, watching to see if his clues were ever solved? Support your opinion with passages from the text.

Writing Prompts

1. Astrid and Quinn's homework assignment was to write about their families and how they came to live in Somerville. Do the same—what is your family's history? How long has your family lived in your town or city, and how did your relatives get there?

2. The townspeople helped Dirk and his friends find the clues without Dirk having to solve the puzzles himself. Have you ever experienced an unfair situation? Write about it!

3. Write a story with Mick as the main character. It can be a story about the diner, a tale about putting together the treasure hunt, or even a retelling of his matchmaking skills. Use what you know about Somerville and the people who live there to make the characters come off the page.

Solve all the SOMERVILLE Mysteries!

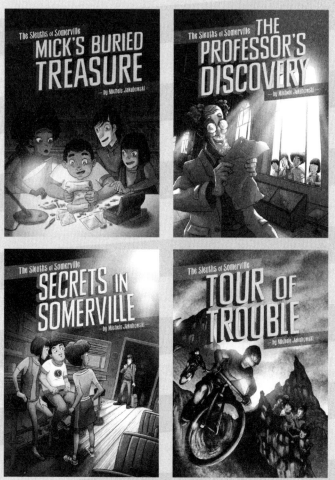